TREASURES of C

W0008492

MEET HATTIE

BOOK 1 OF
THE HATTIE COLLECTION

Marie Hibma Frost

Colorado Springs, Colorado

Meet Hattie

Copyright © 1994 by Marie Hibma Frost
All rights reserved. International copyright secured.

Library of Congress Cataloging-in-Publication Data
Frost, Marie.
    Meet Hattie / Marie Hibma Frost.
        p. cm. — (Hattie series : 1)
    Summary: Hattie Hart is a young girl growing up on a farm in
the 1920s with her Dutch immigrant parents and her brothers and sisters.
        ISBN 1-56179-214-4
    [1. Farm life—Fiction. 2. Family life—Fiction. 3. Dutch
Americans—Fiction.] I. Title. II. Series: Frost, Marie. Hattie
series; 1.
PZ7. F9216Me 1994
[Fic]—dc20   94-10280
                                                       CIP
                                                        AC

Published by Focus on the Family Publishing,
Colorado Springs, Colorado, 80995
Distributed by Word Books, Dallas, Texas

Editor: Etta Wilson
Designer: Harriette Bateman
Interior illustration: Buford Winfrey
Cover Design: Jeff Stoddard

Printed in the United States of America
94 95 96 97 98 99/10 9 8 7 6 5 4 3 2 1

*I dedicate this book
to my husband Eugene*

and

*to our five children:
Sharon, Linda, Eugene, Jr.,
Kaye and Mark*

*for their loving support and
encouragement. This book is a
tribute to the heritage
of their ancestors.*

Some Words You May Need to Know

praten . . . . . . .idle talk or chatter
ya . . . . .yes
kop . . . . .head
fanka . . . . .girl
dominie . . . . . .a pastor
houspisook . . .an occasion when the rulers
in the church come to visit
a home and ask children
questions about their
Christian faith

CONTENTS

Chapter 1

The Lavender Dress

*T*he first thing Hattie saw when she opened her eyes was *her new dress*. It was beautiful! It was the perfect dress for the first day of school.

The night before Hattie had fallen asleep remembering the hot summer day she went with Dad to McGowan's General Store. They had gone to pick up flour, sugar, and a few other things for her mother.

"Go find a flour sack with a print you like," Dad said. "Your mother is going to make you a new dress for school."

As soon as she saw it, she knew it was *the perfect sack* to make *the perfect dress*.

"I like that one!" she cried, pointing up high. "The one with the tiny flowers. Are they purple or blue? I can't tell."

Mr. McGowan looked at Dad and they had both

smiled. "That's the latest fashion color, just in from Paris," Mr. McGowan boasted. "It's called *lavender*."

At home Hattie had watched the flour sack every baking day in hopes it would soon be empty. Finally Mom poured the last of the flour into the big jar she kept in the kitchen. Hattie had grabbed the sack and danced around the kitchen singing, "Lavender blue, dilly dilly, lavender green."

Lavender. Hattie let the word slip from her tongue as she stared at the dress from her bed. She snuggled beneath the covers and imagined her teacher. Hattie knew she would be pretty and delicate, just like the lace collar Mom had made for her wonderful dress.

What was her teacher's name? Hattie thought for a moment. *Miss Henry, that's it. Why, thank you, Miss Henry*, Hattie pretended. *I'm so pleased that you like my dress. The color? Oh, it's lavender, the new color from Paris, of course.*

Hattie felt more grownup already. Even silly old Arnold Best from the farm down the road would notice how grownup she was this year.

"Oh, please, God," Hattie whispered, "don't let Arnold be in my class."

"Hattie! Kathryn!" Mom called up the stairs. "Get up, my two schoolgirls." Across the bed, Hattie's older sister sat up and rubbed her eyes.

Hattie leaped from her side of the bed. With one swoop, she threw the sheet and coverlet over the

She pulled the dress off the hanger and flung it over her head.

feather bed and tossed her pillow on top. After giving it a quick pat, she danced across the room to her dress.

She touched the lace collar gently. Then she pulled the dress off the hanger and flung it over her head.

"Do you think it will be cold in school today, Hattie?" Kathryn laughed as she pointed.

Hattie looked down to see her nightgown sticking out from under her dress. She made a face and stomped her foot. Quickly she tried to remove the dress and nightgown—at the same time. Both came off her body in a tangle and she threw them to the floor.

"Hattie, Hattie," Kathryn sighed and got up. "Always in a hurry." She bent and picked up the tangled mess. Both girls dressed quickly. This time Hattie put her clothes on in the right order.

So much for feeling grownup, Hattie thought.

Mom's voice came up the stairs again. "Breakfast!" she called in her Dutch accent.

"Coming," the two girls answered in one voice. Kathryn tried to pat Hattie's flyaway blonde hair into place as they hurried downstairs.

The rest of the family was already seated at the long, sturdy table. Dad sat at the head of the table. Baby Ervin was babbling in his high chair. Next to him were Leona, almost five, and Clarence, going on eight. Pierce, the oldest boy, sat at Dad's right. Mom came from the kitchen carrying a big plate heaped with eggs and bacon. She sat down at the end of the table near the kitchen.

Dad silently opened the big, black Bible as the girls took their places. "This is the day that the Lord hath made. Let us rejoice and be glad it in," he read in his most reverent voice.

Hattie loved listening to Dad read. When he had come to the United States from Holland as a young man, he knew no English at all.

He finished the psalm, folded his hands, and the whole family bowed their heads. As he began to pray, Hattie said her own silent prayer. Still thinking of her new dress, she prayed she wouldn't spill any juice on it during breakfast.

"Amen!" Hattie called out as she finished her prayer. "Oh, excuse me," she muttered when she heard her brother, Pierce, choke down a giggle. *Another mistake already this morning*, she thought.

Dad shot a stern look at Hattie before he finished praying. Then Mom passed the bacon and eggs to him and the meal began.

Hattie couldn't wait for breakfast to be over. All she could think of was climbing on the yellow school bus and seeing her friends from last year.

Finally everyone was almost ready. Kathryn sat waiting for Mom to braid her hair, and Pierce watched at the window for the school bus.

Hattie twirled round and round in front of the parlor window and sang to the tune of "Happy Birthday."

Happy school day to me,

Happy school day to me,

Happy school day, dear Hattie,

Happy school day to me.

She stopped beside her sister's chair. "Soon I'll be as old as you, Kathryn."

"I will always be older than you," corrected Kathryn.

Hattie paid no attention to her sister. Hattie knew she was older and smarter than last year. And even though she had made a few mistakes this morning, she was sure God gave her a clean slate with each new day.

"I still have my own desk with my name on it," Hattie said, still twirling.

She grabbed a strand of Kathryn's hair and began twirling it too, as she made up a new verse:

I'm braiding your hair,

I'm braiding your hair,

I'm making you pretty

I'm braiding your hair.

12

"Mom!" Kathryn called. "Please come and braid my hair before Hattie gets it all tangled!"

Mrs. Hart hurried into the living room, baby Ervin toddling along behind her. Hattie was sitting in a chair, gazing innocently up at the ceiling.

"What is this *praten* about mussing hair, Miss Hattie?" Mom often spoke in Dutch when she felt hurried or upset.

"I was only trying to help," Hattie replied. "How will I ever learn to braid if no one teaches me?"

"*Ya*," Mom said nodding her head. She turned to Kathryn. "Now keep your *kop* still," she said as her fingers flew through Kathryn's hair, weaving a neat smooth braid.

"The bus is coming around the corner!" Pierce announced just as Mom tightened the ribbon at the end of Kathryn's braid.

"Go! Go! No lunch pails today," Mom called. "School will only last until noon."

Hattie grabbed a yellow pencil and stuffed it in the pocket of her beautiful new lavender dress. She sprinted toward the door, only to slip on Ervin's blanket and fall to the floor with a thump.

That's another mistake, Hattie thought, *and all because of hurrying!*

Chapter 2

A New Friend

*T*he bus rolled into view and stopped in a cloud of dust. Hattie hopped on last, right behind Kathryn, Pierce, and Clarence.

From her seat she watched the familiar white farmhouse fade out of sight. Something in her stomach, no, closer to her heart, felt funny. She almost wanted to cry. She always felt this way as the school year began.

"Hattie, Hattie, drives me batty!" called a voice from the seat right behind her.

"Arnold Best, you're a pest!" Hattie shot back, proud to use a new phrase she had thought up over the summer.

"We're in the same class this year," Arnold said, flashing his lopsided grin. Arnold was older than Hattie, but he had missed a lot of school while helping on his family's farm.

"Good," Hattie said, as sweetly as she could. "Then you'll get to see how smart I am!"

It seemed Hattie had no sooner lost sight of her house than she saw the two-story red schoolhouse ahead. There was the big playground to the side, but Hattie wasn't sure how much time her class this year would have to go out and play.

Even though God had seen fit to put Arnold Best in her class, Hattie didn't mind. There were so many fun things to do—stories, singing, games. She was very excited as she walked down the hall to the fourth grade room.

"I'm Miss Henry," her teacher greeted her at the door.

Hattie looked up and nodded, but she was suddenly too shy to say anything.

Miss Henry was pretty—under her wire-rimmed glasses and dark curly hair—but not in a delicate way. Hattie felt sorry that Miss Henry had a boy's name, but she had a kind voice and a nice smile. Hattie liked her immediately.

"Don't sit next to me, Hattie Hart," Arnold called in a loud voice. "That purple dress might clash with my shirt!"

"I won't," Hattie retorted. "I'd rather stand up than sit by you. And my dress is not purple. It's lavender!"

As Hattie walked down the row, she looked for her name written on a desk. There it was—except there was a new girl already sitting there! Bouncy golden curls covered the girl's head, and she had rosy red cheeks. Her dress was trimmed with ruffles and store-bought lace. Hattie was glad to be wearing her beautiful lavender dress, and even more glad Mom hadn't made her cover it up with her awful brown wool pinafore.

Hattie stopped in front of the desk. She was about to tell the girl to move when she spoke.

"My name is Ruthie Rhenn," she said with a smile.

Hattie was tempted to make up a new name for herself. "Hattie Hart" didn't sound half as pretty as Ruthie Rhenn. Hattie almost introduced herself as "Madeline Lavender", but decided Ruthie would learn her real name soon enough. Besides, Hattie knew it was a sin to lie.

"Mine is Hattie Hart, and you're sitting—"

"Right behind you—I know." Ruthie pointed to Hattie's name on the seat of the desk. Hattie had been looking for names in the wrong place!

Ruthie thought Hattie had a perfectly fine name. The way she said it, it sounded almost as good as Madeline!

Hattie began to tell Ruthie about all the things they would study at school, especially reading and penmanship which were Hattie's favorites. Then Miss Henry came to the front of the room and the girls knew it was time to listen.

"Music always makes me feel happy," said Miss Henry. "I thought we would start each day by singing

America, the Beautiful." Her voice was as smooth as the pages of the Sears & Roebuck catalog as she led the students in singing.

Oh, beautiful for spacious skies,

For amber waves of grain

For purple mountains' majesty

Above the fruited plain . . .

When they finished, Miss Henry gave the class some rules for the year. "Let's remember to raise our hands if we wish to talk," she finished. "Now we will start our math lesson."

After arithmetic it was time for recess. Miss Henry took the class outside to play a game of "Drop the Handkerchief." She had everyone stand in a circle and then chose Curtis Carpenter to be "it." He took the large red bandanna and walked around and around the circle. Suddenly he dropped it behind Arnold Best. Arnold tried to catch Curtis before he got back to the empty space in the circle, but Curtis made it. Next Arnold was "it" and the game continued.

Hattie waited and waited for someone to drop the handkerchief behind her, and finally someone did— the new girl, Ruthie. But the handkerchief fell in the space between Hattie and Clara, and they both stooped to pick it up at the same time.

"It was back of me!" yelled Clara.

"No, it wasn't. It was back of me!" Hattie protested, not about to give up her chance to run around the circle. The girls pulled so hard on the handkerchief, Miss Henry thought it would rip.

"Girls, girls!" Miss Henry scolded. "There will be no fighting."

As if her scolding wasn't bad enough, she then asked Ruthie to take the handkerchief back and choose someone else—neither Hattie nor Clara!

When the school day ended, Hattie didn't want to say good-bye to Ruthie, but she was looking forward to getting home and telling her family all about her new friend.

"I didn't fidget, not even once, and I met a new friend!" she proudly announced to Kathryn and Pierce on the bus.

"Good for you," Kathryn said.

"You only get half credit for not fidgeting today since it was only a half day," Pierce said. "We'll see how you do tomorrow."

"Tomorrow I will be double-good because school will be twice as long," Hattie answered.

The words tumbled from her mouth as she told her brother and sister about her new friend Ruthie and her new teacher Miss Henry.

The next thing Hattie knew, Kathryn was standing up. "Hattie! Hattie! It's time to get off the bus!"

Hattie jumped up with a start and bolted down the aisle. She didn't see Arnold Best stick his foot out, but she heard him laugh as she stumbled off the bus. She looked up and saw Arnold grinning through the window.

Mom was waiting for a report from their first day. "How was school?" she asked as they reached the front porch.

"It was perfect, except for mean old Arnold Best, of course." Hattie yawned. "I'll tell you about my new friend, Ruthie, during lunch. But first I want to change my new dress."

Soon Hattie was sitting on her bed in her white petticoat looking at the new lavender dress she had tossed on the chair. As she leaned over to take off her new black high-top shoes she decided to put her head down for just a minute. Soon she was fast asleep—dreaming of her next day at school and her new friend, Ruthie Rhenn.

Ruthie's Visit

*E*ven before the sun came up on Saturday, Hattie was wide awake with excitement. It was the end of the first week of school, and Mom had said Ruthie could come and play with her today. Hattie hurried to dry the dishes so she would be finished with her work before Ruthie arrived.

Ruthie's dad dropped her off soon after breakfast. Hattie opened wide the door as Ruthie came up the walk. "Want to see what kind of house I live in?" she asked.

Ruthie smiled and nodded. She followed Hattie around the big Hart farmhouse. Ruthie lived in town, so everything about the farm was different and exciting.

When they came to the kitchen, Hattie's mom stopped her work of making bread and greeted Hattie's new friend. Ruthie looked at the huge bowl Mrs. Hart had filled with a puffy mountain of slippery white dough.

"What is that?" asked Ruthie. At Ruthie's house they bought bread at the store.

"It's bread dough," said Hattie. "Sometimes Mom gives us a piece of dough and we can make our own little cookies." She turned to her mother. "Mom, may Ruthie and I make bread cookies?"

Mom smiled and gave Hattie a little piece of the dough. Hattie rolled it out flat with the rolling pin. Then she gave Ruthie the top of the baking powder can and showed her how to cut circles in the dough. Hattie used a thimble to cut tiny circles.

When they had cut all they could, the girls gathered the scraps and Hattie let Ruthie roll the dough. They cut circles until the last piece of dough was used. Then they laid all the circles on a cookie sheet and sprinkled sugar carefully on each one. Mom put the pan in the hot oven.

"I'll show you the rest of our house while the cookies are baking," offered Hattie. She led the way to the dining room. The table there was even bigger than the one in the kitchen. "We eat in here when we have company, and I always practice my writing and spelling in this room," Hattie said.

"And here's the parlor," she pointed as she stepped through the door. "We're not allowed to play in here. This is for company only, and for when the preacher or the elder comes to visit and to ask us questions."

"What kind of questions?" asked Ruthie.

"Oh," said Hattie, "things like `Do you go to the movies? Do you like to dance?,' and `Do you play cards?'"

"Your preacher sounds very strict," said Ruthie, who attended a church that didn't have so many rules.

Hattie nodded and continued her tour. "Mom and Dad's bedroom is next door to the parlor, but we can't see it now because my little brother Ervin is in there taking a nap. I'll show you the rooms upstairs. We have three bedrooms and a spare room."

"That's not very many with all the kids who need a place to sleep," Ruthie said.

"Three of us girls sleep in a room," Hattie explained.

She led Ruthie to her room. "Kathryn and I sleep together and Leona sleeps in a single bed. The boys sleep in the other bedrooms, but their rooms are so messy we won't look at them."

Ruthie wondered what kind of mess the boys made. She didn't have any brothers.

Hattie pointed to the steep stairs that led to the attic. "We can't go up there. Mom won't let us. She stores too many secrets up there. We don't heat the spare room either, but we can look." Hattie opened the door just a crack and sniffed longingly.

Boxes of apples and prunes and sweet-smelling raisins lined one wall. Braids of dried onions and

"I'll show you the rooms upstairs."

bouquets of faded green herbs were tied to the rafters. Big blocks of cheese were aging in pans with wooden lids. A few early pumpkins were piled in one corner waiting to be made into Thanksgiving pie.

Ruthie's tour of the Hart house ended just in time. Both girls smelled their sweet treats baking as they came down the stairs.

"Cookie time," Hattie sang as she and Ruthie clattered quickly into the kitchen. They took the hot cookies outside to eat on the back steps.

"I wish I had lots of brothers and sisters and a big house like you have," Ruthie said longingly.

"I wish you did too," said Hattie. Wanting to cheer Ruthie, she said, "Come with me. I have a surprise to show you."

Hattie wanted to show her Kathryn's little pet chick, Peeper, but Peeper was nowhere to be found. They looked everywhere—in the chicken coop, in the yard, in the barn.

"Maybe it hid under the porch," said Ruthie. As they came around the side of the house, they could hear someone crying.

Clarence was sitting on the front steps, sobbing as he held in his hands Kathryn's little pet chick. "I did it. I killed her, but I didn't mean to!" Clarence cried, louder than ever. "She ran under the rocker while I was rocking and I . . .I kind of—smashed her."

Hattie didn't take time to comfort Clarence.

Instead, she opened the front door and hurried to tell Kathryn what had happened. Kathryn picked up her little chick. It was no longer warm and cuddly. She had a sad, faraway look in her eyes.

Hattie was afraid that Kathryn would burst into tears. "We'll have to have a funeral and bury Peeper," she announced.

Clarence quickly got Dad's shovel. Ruthie, Hattie, Clarence, and Kathryn, holding little Peeper, walked toward the grove to choose a spot for the burial.

"We need a box to bury it in," said Kathryn when they were halfway to the grave site. "Hattie, run back and get one of Dad's empty cigar boxes."

Hattie ran to the house, glad that she could have a part in the funeral.

As Clarence was about to put the box with Peeper in the ground, Kathryn said, "People always pray at a funeral. Hattie, will you pray?"

Hattie, taken by surprise, bowed her head and started to pray, "Lord, bless this food—"

Before she could finish, Kathryn whispered, "Pray your bedtime prayer."

Hattie began again in a solemn voice. "Now I lay me down to sleep." She finished the prayer, and Clarence placed the cigar box holding Peeper in the hole he had dug.

While Clarence threw dirt on top of the box, the girls gathered wildflowers to place on the grave.

Hattie had one more thought. "We need to sing 'Praise God from whom all blessings flow.' It was the most dramatic song Hattie knew. Dad sang it so often around the house that all the children knew it.

"We'll sing it as we march in single file from the grave," said Kathryn.

The procession moved slowly across the yard, each of them singing.

Praise God from whom all blessings flow.

Praise Him all creatures here below.

Praise Him above ye heavenly host.

Praise Father, Son, and Holy Ghost.

It was the highest tribute Hattie could think of for little Peeper. And Ruthie would always remember her first visit to Hattie's house.

Chapter 4

Selling Seeds for Dishes

*T*he *Capper's Weekly* lay on the kitchen table. Hattie looked quickly to see if one of her poems was printed in the paper. Mom had been sending them to the editor.

As she went through the pages, she saw an advertisement in large print:

WIN A PONY OR A SET OF DISHES FOR 12.

The Harts already had a horse, so Hattie wasn't interested in a pony. But a set of dishes for twelve was exactly what Mom could use. Hattie continued to read:

FINE CHINA. BEAUTIFUL JAPANESE FLOWERS ON DAINTY CUPS AND SAUCERS. ORDER YOUR SEEDS TODAY AND LEARN HOW EASY IT IS TO

WIN ONE OF THESE PRIZES. NO MONEY
NEEDED UNTIL SEEDS ARE SOLD.

I'm going to order those seeds today and surprise Mom,
Hattie thought. Quickly she found a pencil and wrote
her order to the address given.

Each day she watched for the mailman. When the
seeds came, she was the proud owner of 144 packages
of vegetable and flower seeds!

"All I have to do," Hattie told Clarence excitedly,
"is sell these seeds and send in the money, and the
prize will be mine. It will be easy," she boasted.

The next day at school she asked Ruthie to help her,
but Ruthie wasn't sure she wanted to do that. "Do
you really think people will buy seeds from us?" she
asked.

"Lots of people plant gardens," Hattie replied.
"They have to buy seeds." She continued eagerly, "It
will be easy. We'll go to a house, knock on the door,
and whoever answers it will say yes or no. Anytime
they say yes, we make money for my mom's new set
of dishes."

"But it's not springtime. People don't plant gardens
now," Ruthie said.

"I know that, but they like to plan their gardens all
winter. We're just helping them get started," replied
Hattie.

Ruthie was still not excited about selling seeds, but
she agreed to help Hattie. That Friday night Hattie

stayed at Ruthie's house. On Saturday they planned to knock on every door in the town of Harris.

The next morning the two salesgirls stood at the door of their first house. Ruthie put the box with seeds in it down by the door and Hattie knocked. A young lady came to the door.

"Do you want to buy some seeds for your garden?" asked Ruthie.

"No, I don't think so," answered the lady. "I don't plan to have a garden next year."

"How about some flower seeds?" asked Ruthie cheerfully.

"Too busy with the kids to think about flowers," said the lady.

Ruthie saw several small faces peeping around the doorway.

"I understand," said Ruthie kindly. "And thank you very much for your time."

After the door had closed, Hattie said, "Ruthie, I'm not sure you did that right. Watch me sell something at the next house."

Hattie knocked on the door. A tired-looking lady answered. She was nicely dressed, but Hattie thought she seemed lonely.

"Good morning," said Hattie brightly. "I see a plant in your window. Do you like flowers?" Not stopping for an answer, Hattie held out a packet of seeds. "Would you be interested in buying some flower seeds?"

The lady hesitated.

"I'm trying to make enough money to buy a set of dishes for my mother," said Hattie. "My friend is helping me."

The lady's face softened. "That is very thoughtful of you," said the woman. "I think I might need some flower seeds next spring after all."

While Hattie told the lady about her big family and the cracked dishes her mother was using, the woman became more and more interested. She not only bought flower seeds, but several packages of vegetable seeds as well. Ruthie was impressed.

"From here on," Ruthie said as they went to the next house, "I'll carry the box of seeds and you sell them."

Hattie went from door to door and store to store. Her selling skills were so good that she sold seeds to almost everyone. The more she told the story about her family's needing dishes, the worse it got. Her mother hardly had a piece of china that wasn't cracked or chipped!

Ruthie finally challenged Hattie. "I've been to your house several times," said Ruthie. "I never noticed that your dishes were all cracked and chipped."

"Maybe I do get a little carried away," Hattie answered, "but you have to admit, we only have one set of plain, old white dishes, and some of those are chipped."

Hattie's best sales results came from Mr. McGowan at the local grocery store. Mr. Hart's big family needed lots of groceries. Mr. McGowan couldn't risk losing a good customer, so he bought lots of seeds.

Hattie stayed at Ruthie's house every night she could. There was always an hour or two after school that Mrs. Rhenn let them go around town to sell seeds. On the days that Hattie was at home, she rushed through her chores so she could head off to a neighbor's house with her box of seeds.

Mrs. Broderick, who lived just up the road, was especially moved by Hattie's appeal. To think the Harts didn't own a proper set of dishes!

She shared her concern with several ladies of the church. "The Harts must have fallen on hard times," she told them after Hattie's visit. "I feel our church's mission efforts should start at home. What can we do to help?"

"I noticed a special on dishes in the Sears catalog," said Mrs. Koostra. "I'd be glad to make a contribution."

"So will I," said Mrs. Post. "The Harts are always first to help anyone in need. Now it's time for us to help them."

Two weeks later, the mailman drove all the way up the Harts' driveway instead of leaving their mail in the box by the road. He took three large packages out of his car and set them on the porch.

"They're from Sears & Roebuck," Mom said, reading the labels. "Nobody here ordered anything from the catalog."

But the label was addressed to Mrs. Nick Hart. Puzzled, Mom opened one of the packages. It was a set of dishes! In the three packages were enough dishes to make a complete set for twelve.

"There must be some mistake," said Mom. "I don't know who could have ordered these dishes." Then she found the note:"We hope you can use these. We are glad to help in time of need." The note wasn't signed.

Now Mom was really puzzled. "I haven't told anybody I needed dishes," she said.

The rest of the family tried to help her clear up the mystery. "Maybe Aunt Minnie from Orange City thought we needed some new dishes," said Kathryn. "She's the only relative who's rich enough to buy them."

"She would have signed her name," said Pierce. "She always wants credit for anything she does."

Hattie kept very quiet.

Several days later the mailman brought another package to the Harts. It was addressed to Hattie.

"Look, Hattie," her mother said. "The box is marked fragile."

Hattie smiled but she didn't say anything. Her prize for selling seeds had finally come.

Carefully she opened the box and started to unwrap the contents. It was the prettiest set of dishes she'd ever seen. There were tiny flowers on each cup and saucer. The plates were the most beautiful of all. They had Japanese ladies dancing with parasols.

"Here, Mom, these are yours," she said excitedly.

Mom was more surprised than ever. Another set of dishes? Now she had two sets of dishes for twelve. The pattern on this one was so delicate she'd hesitate to use them except for special company.

"Hattie," said Mom with tears in her eyes, "you are very kind. But I wonder where the first set of dishes came from?"

No one could even begin to solve the mystery, and Hattie wasn't about to explain anything.

Chapter 5

Cinderella's Stepsister

*O*ne Friday at the close of school, Miss Henry stood before the class. "When you come back to school on Monday, I will choose one of your favorite stories, she announced."We will make a play from the story."

All that weekend Hattie and Ruthie tried to guess which book Miss Henry had chosen.

"I wish we could do Little Red Riding Hood," said Ruthie.

"I hope she picks Sleeping Beauty," declared Hattie. She thought how elegant she would look as the beautiful sleeping princess.

On Monday afternoon Miss Henry waited until it was time to go home. Then she told the class, "I have chosen Cinderella for our play.

All the boys turned up their noses, but the girls giggled with delight.

"Aw, Miss Henry," Arnold Best whined, "can't we do something exciting like Puss in Boots?"

"How about The Three Pigs?" asked Curtis Carpenter. "You won't need a costume, Arnold!"

Miss Henry didn't like the boys to make fun of each other, and she put a quick stop to the teasing. "Cinderella is an exciting story with lots of different parts," she told the class.

Hattie raised her hand. "Miss Henry, do you know who will play Cinderella?"

"After school, I will make a list of who will play each character and you can see it first thing in the morning," she promised.

On the bus going home, Hattie's thoughts turned again to the play. Arnold Best wasn't on the bus, and it was much quieter than usual.

As Hattie did her chores after school at home, she used the time to practice being Cinderella—just in case. When she dusted her bedroom, she swirled and danced around the bed and dresser. She went to the closet and looked at her new lavender dress. I might get to wear this dancing with the handsome prince, she thought.

When she ran down the stairs to dust the parlor, Hattie pretended she was going down the palace steps, trying to reach her coach before it turned back to a pumpkin.

After her own chores were done, she decided to help Pierce and Clarence sweep up straw in the barn. She practiced a slow, sad sweeping motion . . . the way Cinderella would sweep while her sisters were at the prince's ball.

All of a sudden Hattie heard a noise outside the barn.

"Hattie," Arnold Best called. "Why are you practicing to be Cinderella? Don't you know your feet are too big for that part?"

Arnold had been watching Hattie playact through the barn door. Hattie wanted to ignore Arnold, but she also wanted to talk about the play. She stuck her head out of the barn.

Arnold was leaning against a fence post, chewing on a piece of straw.

"Ask me what I know about the play," said Arnold.

"What do you know about the play?" Hattie asked.

"I know who got which part," Arnold said calmly.

"Arnold Best," Hattie exclaimed. "we aren't supposed to find out about the parts until tomorrow!"

"It was such a nice day, I decided to walk home from school," Arnold began in a slow voice. He was trying to stretch the story out as long as he could to keep Hattie in suspense. "Since I was walking home anyway, I stayed after school until Miss Henry wrote the list on the blackboard. After she left, I snuck in and took a quick peek."

Suddenly Hattie's attitude changed. Arnold knew which part she had, and she would have to treat him just right to find out.

39

All of a sudden Hattie heard a noise outside the barn.

"That was pretty brave," Hattie said. "You could've been caught by the principal!"

"I guess, but it was worth it to see your part. I'll tell you what it is if you promise to give me anything I want from your lunch pail for a week," Arnold replied.

Hattie pondered this offer for a moment. Then she crossed her fingers behind her back and made the promise.

Arnold removed the straw from his mouth to make the important announcement. "You, Hattie Hart," he began, "are one of the ugly, mean stepsisters!"

Hattie's mouth dropped open in surprise. *All the ugly stepsisters do is complain and mutter under their breath about Cinderella,* Hattie thought.

"Arnold," Hattie warned. "If you're lying, may God strike you dead with lightning!"

Hattie looked hopefully at the sky, but all she saw was a few puffy clouds.

"Have fun with your part," Arnold teased. "At least you won't have to practice being ugly!"

Hattie wanted to cry. She picked up a chunk of dried mud and hurled it toward Arnold's head. He stood still as the clod sailed straight over his head. Then he laughed and made a face at Hattie before he turned to run home.

Right then and there, Hattie decided she would make the best of her part. She would show Arnold Best.

On the bus the next morning, Hattie kept her fingers crossed. She hoped Arnold had been lying, and that she would be Cinderella or at least the fairy godmother.

When she arrived at school, she found Ruthie twirling and dancing near the blackboard where the parts were written.

"Can you believe it?" Ruthie giggled. "Miss Henry chose me to be Cinderella. I'm so excited, I don't know what to do."

Yes, Hattie could believe it. Ruthie was the most beautiful girl in class, with her bouncy blonde curls and honey-brown eyes. Even though Ruthie was her best friend, Hattie sometimes wished Ruthie weren't so beautiful and sweet.

When all the class was seated, Miss Henry handed out scripts for them to take home and learn. She also gave Ruthie a song to practice, and Curtis Carpenter, the prince, a poem to recite.

Some of the boys were happy that they would play the mice that turn into horses for Cinderella's coach. Arnold Best was happy that he didn't have a part after Miss Henry found out he had sneaked into the room the afternoon before. But Ruthie Rhenn was happiest of all, because she would be Cinderella!

That evening, Hattie sat thinking of how she could make her part better. *I can sing just as well as Ruthie,* thought Hattie, *if not better. I know, I'll write a song to sing in the play.* She began to sing:

> *I'm a mean, ugly stepsister, that is true,*
>
> *But now is my chance to try on the glass shoe.*
>
> *I hope it fits so the prince marries me.*
>
> *Then what a beautiful bride I will be.*

Hattie asked Kathryn to help her write the music with words so she would remember them. "I'll show the song to Miss Henry tomorrow," she said.

To Hattie's delight, Miss Henry loved her song and put it in the play.

After several weeks of practicing and making costumes and decorating the stage, the play was ready to present. Ruthie couldn't wait to wear her Cinderella costume.

"Don't you love the pink color?" she asked Hattie. "And the little sequins around the neck? My mother made it."

"I'm going to wear a fake green wart on the tip of my nose," declared Hattie. "Look at the ugly face I can make. Don't laugh! I've been practicing for weeks. It isn't my natural face, you know."

Ruthie couldn't stop laughing. "You'll probably do your part better than I'll do mine!" Ruthie said.

Finally the night of the play arrived. The mice wanted to show off and went in all directions. The other ugly stepsister lost the bow for her hair and forgot the only line she had to say in the play. Curtis, who was the prince, was so shy he was afraid to look at Ruthie.

When the prince came near the door to the stepsisters' house, Hattie knew her big moment had come. It was time for her to sing.

As her family, friends, and neighbors watched, Hattie took a deep breath and sang as clearly as she had ever sung in her life.

I'm a mean, ugly stepsister, that is true,

But now is my chance to try the glass shoe.

I hope it fits so the prince marries me,

Then what a beautiful bride I will be.

"All he'll see is those big feet!" Arnold Best suddenly crowed from the audience.

Ripples of laughter swept through the audience. Hattie's face turned red. She didn't think he was funny at all! Now everyone knew that she had big feet, and Arnold had ruined her singing debut! Thank goodness the play was almost over.

After the play, cookies and punch were served, but they didn't look good to Hattie. All she could feel in the pit of her stomach was anger toward Arnold Best and toward whoever wrote Cinderella in the first place.

Imagine, writing a book with so many mean and ugly characters, she thought. *I'm going to write my own books someday with only good characters, so no one else will have to go through what I did!*

"Do you want something to eat?" asked Ruthie as she handed Hattie a cup of punch and a napkin filled with cookies. "I grabbed these for you before the boys ate everything."

"Thanks," Hattie said. She nibbled on a cookie as Ruthie talked.

"The play was wonderful, wasn't it?" Ruthie sighed. "All except for my song. Oh, Hattie, how I wish I could sing like you! You sang your song so well!"

Hattie had been so busy pouting over Arnold's comment that she hadn't thought about the good things in the play. She had sung well. Miss Henry had told her so after the play.

Soon Pierce, Kathryn, Mom, and Dad, and all the Hart family were standing around Hattie.

"You were pretty good," said Pierce.

"A born actress," Kathryn agreed.

"I was so proud of you," added Dad.

45

"You know, Hattie," Mom said, "everybody wants to play the fancy parts, but it is hard to play the part that is not like you really are, my lovely fanka."

Hattie smiled and finished her cookie. That terrible feeling in her stomach had suddenly disappeared.

Chapter 6

The Fickle Bride

*B*ecause Hattie had been a good helper, her mother didn't mind letting her spend Saturday morning with her friend Ruthie. It was a beautiful fall day, and Hattie was happy as she went with Ruthie to choir practice at her church.

"Would you like to sing with us?" asked Miss Page, who was the director of the children's choir.

"Oh, please do," said Ruthie. "We need all the help we can get, and you're a good singer."

Hattie said a quick prayer to God, just in case it was a sin for her to sing at another church. She waited expectantly, but nothing happened and she decided God must not mind.

When they started singing, Hattie was a little surprised to find that the songs were familiar, and she sang out jubilantly.

"We won't take as much time as usual to practice,"

said Miss Page. "There's a wedding scheduled for this morning, and we need to be out of the building by ten o'clock.

"Dad won't be picking me up for awhile," Hattie told Ruthie. "Why don't we see what a church wedding is like?"

"I've never been to a church wedding," said Ruthie. "But we can't go because we haven't been invited."

"I have an idea," Hattie said. Hattie always seemed to have an idea. "We could go up in the balcony and get behind the railing that has a curtain. If we lie on our stomachs, we can peek through the railing and no one will see us."

Ruthie wondered if her mother would approve.

"Please do it!" urged Hattie.

Unable to think of any hidden dangers, Ruthie agreed. The girls hurried up the stairs to the balcony. They were just getting situated in their hiding place when people started coming into the sanctuary.

The organist took her seat and began playing. Ushers soon began seating guests.

"Isn't this exciting?" whispered Hattie.

After a short time, four men came through a door in the front of the church and stood straight as arrows along the front.

"Which one is getting married?" asked Ruthie.

"I don't know. They all look alike," said Hattie.

48

The organist played more music. Hattie and Ruthie strained their necks to look below and see what would happen next. Three ladies walked slowly in a single file up the center aisle of the church toward the waiting men. They stopped opposite the place where the men were standing.

"Look at those beautiful pink dresses!" said Ruthie.

"And the flowers are pink, too," Hattie whispered. "I never, ever saw anything so beautiful."

Then the organist started playing a new song. It was very loud and sounded very important.

"Look! Look!" said Hattie. "Here come the ones who are getting married!" She pointed to a girl holding on to the arm of a man as they walked slowly down the aisle.

"Look at the sparkling beads on her dress!" said Ruthie. "She looks like a princess!"

Hattie and Ruthie watched the "princess" and her soon-to-be husband walking toward the front of the church. Then the strangest thing happened! "Princess" left the man she was with and picked one of the other men to marry!

Hattie wondered if this was the way people in this church did things. She looked at Ruthie, but Ruthie looked confused too.

"Can't she make up her mind?" whispered Hattie. "The first man must feel terrible that she left him at the last minute."

"Here come the ones who are getting married."

"Maybe she'll go back to the first one before it's over," Ruthie said with a shrug.

But the first man sat down and that was that!

Although Ruthie and Hattie enjoyed watching their very first wedding, they were disappointed in the fickle bride. When the wedding was over and the crowd started to leave, Hattie and Ruthie made a silent getaway.

After Hattie arrived home and the family was seated at the table for supper, Mom asked, "Did you have a nice time today, Hattie?"

"Oh, yes," Hattie said. "I sang in the choir and went to a wedding!"

"Hattie, why do you always have to make up these stories just to impress people?" asked Kathryn.

"Because her imagination works overtime," Pierce teased.

"I did, too, sing in the choir," Hattie said hotly, "but I was just practicing."

"Well, it was a wasted practice, because you won't be singing there Sunday," Pierce said. "You belong to our church."

"How did you go to a wedding dressed in your play clothes?" her mother wondered.

"If you won't get mad, I'll tell you," Hattie replied with a grin.

Everyone promised, wondering what Hattie would tell them. Satisfied that she wouldn't be scolded,

Hattie described how she and Ruthie had ended up as uninvited guests at a church wedding. She included every detail of the wedding, adding to whatever she thought was necessary.

"It was very beautiful, but very, very sad," Hattie concluded dramatically. "The girl—I called her the princess—couldn't decide who she wanted to marry. She came down the aisle with one, but then, as soon as she got up to the front of the church, she picked another one!"

"Whatever are you talking about?" asked Pierce.

Hattie looked around the dinner table. She noticed Mom and Dad smiling, and Kathryn was laughing out loud.

Pierce and Kathryn had been to several church weddings. They knew what had really happened, but Hattie was still bewildered. All Hattie knew was that they were laughing at her!

"Hattie," Dad said kindly, "Let me explain. The first man who walked with your princess down the aisle was her father. He was taking her to her husband. So, you see, she wasn't fickle at all. That's just how weddings go."

Hattie thought about what Dad had said. Things started to make sense to her, and she could see why Pierce and Kathryn had laughed.

"There's never a dull moment with our Hattie around," said Dad, smiling. Hattie couldn't bring herself to smile back. Nobody likes being laughed at and Hattie was still feeling hurt.

Later in the evening, when she was safely tucked in her bed and no one else could hear, Hattie admitted to her doll that she had really had a fun day.

"I'm just glad the princess knew what she was doing," Hattie whispered. Lady Loretta Lavender looked at Hattie wisely, but said nothing. *That's one thing about dolls,* Hattie thought. *They never, ever laugh at you.*

Hattie let her mind drift off to the day her father would walk down the aisle with her, and at last she would get to be a princess.

Chapter 7

Gypsies Come and Go

*T*he Harts were sitting around the table and eating breakfast. Dad had just announced there were gypsies in the neighborhood, and Pierce was teasing his younger sister.

"Gypsies eat kids like you, Hattie," said Pierce.

"How can they eat me? I'm too big," Hattie replied.

"Oh, they will probably fry you with butter in one of their big pans," said Pierce with a grin.

Then Kathryn joined in. "People say that gypsies use charms to put spells on people."

Hattie's eyes opened wide. "Dad, can they make me do things I don't want to?"

"No, they can't do that." Then he added with a smile, "No one can make Hattie do things she doesn't want to do!"

"They'll steal you blind," Pierce said solemnly. He was not sure what that meant, but he had heard someone else say it about gypsies.

That afternoon, Ruthie rode the school bus home with Hattie so the girls could play together. They were on the front porch when they heard the crunching sound of wagon wheels on gravel.

"It's the gypsies! It's the gypsies!" said Hattie when she caught sight of a wagon covered with a dirty, ragged canvas.

Pots and pans of every shape and size clanged against the wagon's worn side. The gypsies made money mending them as they traveled from place to place. Hattie remembered Pierce's threat. Just in case, she looked to see if any pans were her size.

"I wonder if they're going to stop or go right by," said Ruthie fearfully.

But they didn't go right by. They turned in at the Hart gate. A lot of grownups and children tumbled from the wagon. The women had colored bandannas on their heads. They wore long, colorful skirts, beads around their necks, and jangling bracelets on their arms. The children were barefooted and dirty, but they had smiles on their faces.

A very old gypsy man, with most of his teeth missing, came forward. Dad went out to meet him. The old man, who seemed to be the leader of the group, began to show Dad things he wanted to sell. He held up a woven basket.

"How much?" asked Dad.

"I'll trade it for three chickens—healthy ones," added the gypsy with his toothless smile.

Dad knew gypsies liked to bargain. "I'll give you two," he said.

"Sold," said the man. He knew he had asked too much, but that was all part of bargaining.

A gypsy woman brought out a lace tablecloth from one of the wagons. "It is handmade. I crocheted it," she said, smiling. Dad could tell it had been made on a machine, but it was pretty.

"What do you want to trade for that?" asked Dad.

"We need fruits and vegetables," said the woman. She was thinking of all the people she had to feed with her meager soups. "What do you have?"

"We have just finished canning tomatoes. You can have four jars of tomatoes and two bushels of apples from the trees in the grove," offered Dad. "But you'll have to pick the apples yourselves."

The woman handed Dad the tablecloth and the gypsies ran toward the grove.

"Can you watch them, Mom?" asked Dad, giving her the tablecloth. "Make sure they take only two bushels."

Mom was pleased with the tablecloth, but she couldn't afford to lose too many apples. She followed the gypsies to the apple grove.

Hattie and Ruthie had been watching and they weren't frightened anymore. Dad seemed to have everything under control.

"Let's play hide and seek now," said Ruthie.

"I'll be the first one to hide," Hattie said. "Close your eyes, Ruthie. Count to one hundred and don't cheat!"

Hattie decided to hide in the manger in the barn. *She'll never find me here*, Hattie told herself as she snuggled down in the hay.

Ruthie called out "one hundred" and began her search. She looked in the chicken house and the outhouse and all around the big Hart farmhouse, but she couldn't find Hattie. She could see Mrs. Hart, still watching the gypsies as they busily picked their apples. Mr. Hart and Pierce had gone to the fields. But Hattie was not to be seen.

Hattie had been lying in the hay for some time. She was getting tired of waiting to be found. She decided it was time to play something else.

"Ruthie!" Hattie called, brushing the hay from her clothes as she came out of the barn. "I'm over here and you didn't find me!"

Hattie waited a few minutes, but Ruthie didn't appear. The yard was deserted. Even the gypsies had left and Mom had gone back into the house. Hattie looked all around for Ruthie, calling, "Ruthie, Ruthie!"

Maybe she just gave up on finding me and went into the house, thought Hattie. She walked to the kitchen door and went inside. Mom was busy cutting up apples for a pie.

"Have you seen Ruthie?" Hattie asked hopefully.

But Mom hadn't seen Ruthie. Neither had any of the other Hart children. Mom sent Clarence to get Pierce and Dad, and soon the whole Hart family was searching the farm for Ruthie.

"Do you think the gypsies put a spell on Ruthie and took her away?" asked Hattie when their long search had failed to turn up Ruthie. "She's my best friend!"

"If the gypsies did take her, we'll catch up with them," promised Dad. "Pierce, let's hitch up the horses to the wagon and go look for Ruthie."

"I want to go too," said Hattie.

"All right, but you'll have to stay in the wagon," Dad replied. Hattie jumped up and sat behind Pierce.

Dad drove furiously, not sparing the horses. "We'll find them. I think they headed for the river," he told Pierce.

"But I don't see any wheel tracks," said Pierce, who had been watching the road for their trail. "They seem to have disappeared."

Hattie thought she must have traveled miles and miles as she bounced around in the back of the wagon. They looked everywhere, but they found no signs of the gypsies—or of Ruthie.

It was almost dark when they returned to the

Rhenns. Hattie and Pierce stayed in the wagon while Dad went inside to tell them the sad news.

Mr. and Mrs. Rhenn called the sheriff and the search began that very night. Three days passed, but neither Ruthie nor the gypsies were found. Poor Mr. and Mrs. Rhenn were heartbroken. They just stayed in their house, hoping for some good news, not wanting to talk to anyone.

Hattie knew how they felt. Nothing would be any fun anymore without Ruthie. Hattie kept wondering what had happened to her friend.

She prayed that God would help Ruthie find a way to escape from the gypsies. Dad said God never made mistakes, but Hattie wondered how God could let such a thing happen. She just didn't understand. And she really missed Ruthie!

Chapter 8

A Thanksgiving Art Lesson

*H*attie didn't like going to school without Ruthie's being there. She would turn around to smile at Ruthie during a funny story in a book or to make a face when Arnold said something goofy. But when Hattie turned to look, Ruthie wasn't there. Hattie missed Ruthie so much. She thought her heart ached as much as Mr. and Mrs. Rhenns' did. She missed Ruthie as much as if one of her own sisters had been taken away.

As the days passed, Hattie tried to find a new friend to play with. Most of the girls and boys in her class had been together in school since first grade. There were Cletus and Mae, who always stuck together. They had never paid much attention to Hattie.

There was Clara, fat as ever, always huffing and puffing. Beatrice who was smart, but she had no imagination and she wasn't as pretty as Ruthie. Moses, who was freckled and skinny, liked Hattie, but he was too serious. Lola was bossy, Roberta talked too loud and too fast, and Charlotte always told the teacher when Hattie was having a lot of fun. Hattie did like dark-haired Curtis Carpenter and wished he would like her. Would she have to settle for Beatrice as her best friend?

Miss Henry kept reminding the students how grown-up they were. Hattie knew she was grown-up. She also knew she was heartsick over losing her friend Ruthie—and she was bored.

Miss Henry assigned the class reading from books that seemed like first-grade primers to Hattie. She already knew all the words in the books. When it was time to do the writing exercises, she knew all those words too. She broke her pencil lead on purpose so she could get up and go to the pencil sharpener near the window. Hattie would turn the sharpener's crank and look out the window at the grass, trees, and birds. She imagined that one day she would see Ruthie waving at her.

As weeks passed, Hattie became more interested in school. She loved to draw and art class was her favorite. Sometimes she drew pictures to go with the poems she wrote. At home Hattie tacked pictures and poems all over the walls. She even drew pictures for the front of Mom's kitchen cupboards.

November finally came and Miss Henry began to tell the class the story of the first Thanksgiving. "The

Pilgrims came to this land because they wanted to worship God the way they thought best," explained Miss Henry. "They started from England in a ship called the Mayflower, and landed at Plymouth Rock."

Beatrice raised her hand. "If a ship lands on a rock it will sink."

"They didn't land on a rock," Miss Henry explained. "It was a place called Plymouth Rock."

"We have Plymouth Rock chickens at home, but I've never seen them sitting on any rocks," said Arnold.

Miss Henry saw that things were getting out of hand. "Let's get back to the story," she said.

Just when things get interesting, the teachers always change the conversation, Hattie thought.

"The Pilgrims didn't have too much food that first winter," Miss Henry continued. "Some starved to death. The next summer, thanks to the friendly Indians who helped them plant corn, they had good crops.

"What do you think they had to eat at the first Thanksgiving?" asked Miss Henry.

There was a chorus of answers. Leading the list was turkey, followed by pumpkin and cranberries.

"Mashed potatoes," added Clara.

Now that all the children were thinking about Thanksgiving, Miss Henry decided it would be a good time for them to put their ideas into pictures.

"Thanksgiving pictures would make nice decorations for our room. Remember our story? You could draw Pilgrims, Indians, or corn and other kinds of foods. Be original. Think of something no one else will draw."

Hattie raised her hand. "I can show the class how to draw a turkey," she volunteered.

Miss Henry was intrigued. "All right," she said, "Would you like to come to the blackboard?"

Hattie marched to the front of the room and started drawing on the blackboard. "A big round circle with hills all around," she chanted, as she drew a circle with little hills on the top and side.

She continued her rhyme. "A question mark next and two feet on the ground." Hattie drew a question mark for the head and neck and two stick feet at the bottom of the circle.

Hattie, wishing to savor her place of importance, repeated the rhyme as she went over her drawing a second time:

A big round circle

With hills all around,

A question mark next

And two feet on the ground.

64

Then she added some squiggly feathers inside the circle and a small dot inside the question mark for an eye.

"Very nicely done," said Miss Henry. "You will make a good teacher someday."

Hattie seemed to float on air as she returned to her desk. *Just think,* Hattie said to herself, *Miss Henry said I might be a teacher some day—a good teacher.*

The students got out their crayons from their desks. Miss Henry gave each one a large piece of white paper.

"Use your imagination," she said. "After you finish the pictures, we will come to our circle and talk about the different things you have drawn."

The class was quiet while each student drew his or her picture. Then they hurried to the circle of chairs Miss Henry had made at the front of the room, eager to show their works of art.

"Cletus," began Miss Henry, "would you like to show us what you have drawn?"

"It's a turkey," said Cletus, holding up her picture. "But my circle is lopsided."

"It looks friendly," Miss Henry said.

Lola held up her picture next. "Mine's a turkey too," said Lola. "And I like my turkey."

Arnold showed his picture next. Another turkey! "Mine is different," he said. "He was hungry and he is eating some worms."

One student after another held up a picture. All of them had drawn turkeys, very much like the one Hattie had drawn on the blackboard. Skinny turkeys, fat turkeys, little turkeys, big ones, some with lots of feathers, some looking like they had been plucked.

Miss Henry had hoped for more variety in the pictures, but she couldn't help smiling.

"What did you draw, Hattie?" she asked.

Hattie held up her carefully drawn picture of a girl next to her turkey. Everybody could tell it was Ruthie.

"That's what I would like for Thanksgiving—to have Ruthie back," she said.

The Broken Candy Dish

*H*attie had a make-believe friend she called Evelyn Series. Hattie liked the name Evelyn because a singer with that name had come to the town of Harris to perform. Then one day in school Miss Henry had put the word "series" on the blackboard for the class to study. Hattie learned that a series is a group or set of things. She liked that word a lot.

Sometimes Hattie talked to Evelyn in the barn, sometimes in the living room, and sometimes in her room if Kathryn and Leona were not there. Hattie always felt that Evelyn listened to her.

One day Hattie's mom asked her to dust the living room. "The dominie and the elders are coming for houspisook," she said. "I want the parlor to be sparkling clean."

"Why do the minister and those old elders have to come today?" muttered Hattie. "Houspisook is a pain with all those silly questions they ask us. They see us every Sunday. Why don't they check up on us at church?"

"They are godly men trying to be certain you know the ways of our Lord," Mom replied. "I don't want to hear any more about it."

"I want to go outside and play. Pierce just fixed a new tire swing. You always make me wear an apron and work in the house when the boys get to play," protested Hattie.

"That's enough, Hattie Hart. Here's the dusting cloth," Mom said sharply.

Hattie swished the cloth back and forth on the legs of the couch, back and forth across the table next to the couch, and here and there on the rungs of the rocking chair. Just so it looked like she had dusted everything, she swished at the window sill and across the front of the marble table by the window. CRASH! The candy dish on the table swished right to the floor!

Oh, dear, thought Hattie, *Look what I've done. It's Mom's best crystal candy dish! I can't tell her. I know, I'll go to the five-and-ten-cent store and find a dish that looks sort of like this one. Maybe she'll never notice.*

Hattie picked up the sharp jagged pieces and slipped them into her apron pocket. For once she was glad that she was wearing her apron. Hattie thought her problem was solved.

Just then Mom came into the room with a bag of

pink and white peppermints. "Our guests might like some candy when they come for houspisook," she said. "Let's see, where is my good candy dish? Did you see it, Hattie?"

"No, I don't think so," Hattie lied. "I don't know where it is."

Then Mom picked up a piece of broken glass from the floor. As she straightened up, she noticed Hattie's bulging pocket.

"Hattie, are you sure you don't know where the candy dish is?" she asked.

Hattie hung her head and pointed to her pocket. "I broke it, but—"

"Empty your pocket and go to your room now," ordered Mom. "And don't come down until I call you. I am not punishing you because you broke the dish, but because you lied to me about doing it."

Hattie ran up the stairs to her room. She closed the door behind her as hot tears ran down her face. From across the room she could see into the mirror, and she began to talk to Evelyn Series.

"I always get into trouble," Hattie grumbled to her make-believe friend, but she didn't think Evelyn was feeling sorry for her.

Then Hattie picked up her pencil and tablet of paper from the table beside her bed. Writing down her feelings usually made Hattie feel better. *Maybe if I write a poem, it will help,* Hattie thought.

Finally she came up with a poem she liked, except she couldn't think of a last line:

God, you know I didn't mean

To break that candy dish.

It slipped from my fingers

When my dusting cloth went swish.

I'm sorry I told a lie . . .

Let's see, what could I say for the last line? she wondered. Then she scribbled down something that rhymed:

I'll do better by and by.

That wasn't really the way she felt, but writing it down helped her feel better. She put it in her apron pocket and began to talk with Evelyn again.

It seemed like a long, long time before Mom called Hattie down for supper. She could hear the dominie and the elders at the front door when they finally left. Her stomach growled noisily as she hurried down the stairs and sat at the table. All the family was there, waiting for Dad to begin the prayer.

After Dad finished, he looked around the table and said, "I want each of you to say a prayer tonight. Clarence, you go first."

"God is great, God is good, and we thank Him for our food." Clarence said the familiar prayer. Then Kathryn said a prayer of thanksgiving for the good visit of the elders.

It was Hattie's turn next. Suddenly she remembered what was in her pocket. She pulled out the paper and read:

God, you know I didn't mean

To break that candy dish.

It slipped from my fingers

When my dusting cloth went swish.

I'm sorry I told a lie,

but I'll do better by and by. Amen

Hattie looked up and saw a smile on her mom's face. She was glad she had a family that wanted her to do what was right. Hattie felt much better because she knew God did forgive her. Deep down inside she felt safe and happy. She hoped Ruthie was safe too.

Chapter 10

A Cat Named Puzzle

*H*attie kicked at the dirt and blinked back her tears. *Where is Ruthie? I miss her so much,* she thought. Hattie went inside the barn to look for eggs. "I'll just go in and talk to Evelyn Series for a while," she said to herself.

"Evelyn," complained Hattie plunking herself on a hay bale, "nobody else even wants me around. If I weren't here, lots of people would be happy. Pierce would be glad that I wouldn't be tricking him anymore. Kathryn wouldn't have to pick up my clothes in our bedroom. Leona wouldn't have to be worry because I was always getting her in trouble. Clarence could do what he pleased without me to boss him. Ervin might miss me for a while, but he'd soon forget. You're the only one who cares, Evelyn— and you're not even real!"

While Hattie was pouring out her heart to Evelyn,

she felt something soft and furry rubbing against her leg. Realizing it was a kitten, she started to shoo it away. Then she noticed that the cat's tail was missing. It must have been cut off and then healed.

"Oh, you poor thing!" said Hattie as she picked up the kitten. A plain old cat was one thing. A kitten with a problem was something else. "Do you feel sad too?" Hattie whispered, as she cradled the kitten in her arms. The kitten, used to being kicked rather than cuddled, started to purr.

"How did you lose your tail? Did a hay mower run over you?" Hattie asked.

She held the kitten close. It wasn't beautiful. It was sort of a light grey with splotches of black. It reminded Hattie of a puzzle whose pieces didn't fit together. "I think I'll call you Puzzle," she said.

It was time for Hattie to finish her chores. She carefully put Puzzle down on the floor of the barn for the moment. But the kitten had felt good to hold, and she wouldn't forget her new friend.

As the week went by, whenever Hattie was outside, Puzzle ran to her and followed her. When Puzzle wanted to show off for Hattie, she would groom her fur with her little pink tongue. She cocked her ears as if she were listening to every word Hattie said. Then she would look at Hattie as if to say, "Pick me up. Don't you love me?"

"I know how you feel," Hattie told Puzzle. "I miss

my friend Ruthie. I wish someone would pick me up and tell me they love me!"

Mom noticed that Hattie was playing with the kitten a lot. "You can't let Puzzle be a house cat, Hattie. Animals belong outside," she said. Hattie nodded. She knew Mom felt that way.

One evening, when Puzzle scrambled on the front porch to have her dinner, there was a big black tomcat eating from the dish. This would never do! The kitten flattened her ears and hissed to scare away the intruder.

The tomcat hardly noticed Puzzle and kept right on crunching food. Puzzle moved closer to the dish. The annoyed tomcat pounced on Puzzle, clawing and biting the small kitten. Round and round rolled the two cats in the grass. Puzzle felt claws and teeth through her fur. She didn't care about food anymore—she just wanted to get away!

When the big cat left, Puzzle crawled to the back door and gave one weak, desperate "meow." Hattie was in the kitchen and heard the cry. She quickly opened the door.

"Oh, Puzzle! What happened? Look Mom, Puzzle's bleeding!"

Poor Puzzle was a mess. Her ear was torn. She had mud all over her fur and she was bleeding. Hattie ran to get a warm, wet towel to wipe off her kitten.

"Please don't send Puzzle outside!" pleaded Hattie.

"All right, she can stay inside for a while," said Mom. "Put her in a box behind the stove to dry her fur." Mom was still opposed to having a cat in the house, but she said to Hattie, "Every animal needs help sometimes."

Dad was even more against animals in the house than Mom. Hattie had heard him say many times, "Animals belong outside on the farm." But as Puzzle's wounds healed, Dad was the one who became attached to her. The kitten often jumped on Dad's lap at night when he was sitting in his chair reading the paper. Puzzle would nudge at the paper until Dad put the it aside and petted her.

"This kitten isn't such a bad cat," Dad said, ruffling her fur. "And it sure is a smart one."

One night very late, almost morning, Dad awoke to a strange sound. It was a wailing, "M-E-O-W . . . M-E-O-W!" Puzzle was standing on Dad's chest, pawing first with one foot, then the other, frantically trying to wake him.

"Go away, Puzzle. I want to sleep," Dad grumbled, but Puzzle wouldn't stop pawing and meowing. Then Dad smelled smoke! He was wide awake in a second. He jumped out of bed and ran from the bedroom to see where the smoke was coming from.

Through the door in the kitchen, he could see a glowing light flickering, and smoke pouring up from the wood box that stood by the kitchen stove. The wood box was on fire!

Dad quickly opened the lid to the water reservoir at the back of the stove and started scooping out water and throwing it on the fire. Soon the flames died to soggy ashes.

While Dad was busy putting out the fire, Mom ran upstairs with Ervin in her arms. "Wake up! Wake up!" she called to the children. "The house is on fire!"

By the time she had all the children awake and down the stairs, the fire was out.

"Boy! What a lot of smoke!" said Pierce.

"Open the windows and doors," said Dad. "We need to air this place out!"

After a few minutes, most of the smoke was gone. Dad collapsed in his big chair in the kitchen. The children gathered around, wondering what in the world had happened. Dad and the boys were wearing the long winter underwear that they slept in. Mom and the girls stood shivering in their long flannel nightgowns.

"Dad, how did you know there was a fire?" asked Pierce. "How did it start?"

"I never played with matches," said Leona.

"I didn't either," said Clarence.

Dad didn't say anything for a few minutes. Puzzle came into the room and climbed up on Dad's lap.

"Children," Dad said, stroking the cat's fur lovingly, "Puzzle saved our lives tonight. The wood box was on fire and Puzzle came to the bedroom and climbed on my chest and woke me up just in time."

Hattie was thinking of a Bible verse: "Do unto others as you would have them do unto you."

"I'm sure Puzzle never read the Bible," laughed Hattie. "Maybe she wanted to be good to us because because we were good to her."

Mom and Dad smiled at Hattie's wisdom. The children went back upstairs, grateful that the house hadn't burned down with them inside.

As Dad trudged back to bed, he said to Mom, "I knew all the time that cat was smart!"

The Lost Ring

*T*he first day of December came—Hattie's tenth birthday. Her favorite Uncle Garrett in California sent her a birthstone ring. Hattie couldn't wait to get to school to show it to her teacher.

On the day Hattie took her ring, Miss Henry let the class have "show and tell" time. Hattie almost started bouncing. She could hardly wait for her turn. She waved her hand in the air again and again. Finally, Miss Henry called on her.

"Do you see the ring I'm wearing?" she asked as she stood before the class. On her finger was the beautiful silver ring with its vivid blue stone."It's my birthstone," Hattie said proudly.

"Did you steal it?" asked Arnold Best.

"For your information," Hattie answered hotly, "My uncle gave it to me for my birthday."

"Children," Miss Henry cautioned. "If you can't say something that is kind, say nothing. Hattie, can you tell us what kind of stone is in your ring?" Miss Henry asked.

"It's turquoise." Hattie pronounced turquoise very deliberately. She had practiced her new word with Kathryn.

"Is the ring real silver?" asked Clara.

"I don't know, but the stone is real. An Indian in Arizona made the ring."

My birthday is in December too," Arnold piped up. "But I wouldn't wear a ring. I'd take out the stone and add it to my stone collection."

Clara was next to tell something. "My mom had a baby girl last night," she announced.

Oh really, thought Hattie. She was quite used to her mother having a baby about every other year, but she had never thought that was worth saying out loud in school.

Moses was next. "My dad promised to take me sledding during Christmas vacation," he said.

Immediately half the class started waving their hands, wanting to tell what they were going to do during Christmas holidays. The other half were excited by the few flakes of snow falling slowly past the window. Miss Henry had quite a time getting the class to settle down.

"I know you're all thinking about the Christmas

vacation that's coming up," she said, "but we'll have to forget about your vacation. Now it's time to get some work done. Please take out your readers."

Slowly, the children put their hands down and turned away from their thoughts of snowballs and snowmen and snow forts and sleds.

Hattie shook her head. All teachers must be the same. Why do they say such silly things as "forget about your vacation"? It was a lot easier to forget about readers. Hattie sighed out loud.

As soon as she got home from school, Hattie went upstairs to put her ring in the little treasure box she kept near her bed. *I'm going to take special care of my ring*, thought Hattie. *It might get scratched if I wear it while I do my chores.*

Mom had invited Arnold Best and his mother to come over for hot chocolate and sugar cookies that evening. Mrs. Best was a widow and Mrs. Hart knew she must be lonely, especially so close to the holidays. Hattie felt sorry for Mrs. Best too, but she didn't like the idea of goofy Arnold coming over.

That evening Arnold was on his best behavior—maybe because his mother was around. He and Hattie tried playing checkers on the kitchen table, but little Ervin kept pushing the checkers around.

"Let's go upstairs where the little kids won't bother us," said Hattie.

They sat on the floor in the hall and played several

games of checkers without fighting one time.

After a while Mom called Hattie down to help serve the cookies and hot cocoa. Hattie was tired after the Bests left, but she had almost decided Arnold could be nice when he tried.

The next morning, Hattie hurried to dress for school. She decided to ask Mom if she could wear her ring again if she were careful. She opened her treasure box.

"My ring!" she said. "It's gone!" She looked through her box again, but the ring was not there. She looked at her sister across the room. "Kathryn, did you take my ring?" she asked sharply.

"No, I did not take it," Kathryn said. "And I haven't seen it either."

"What about you, Leona?" Hattie asked. "I bet you took it."

"I did not," answered Leona.

"Wait a minute," Hattie said loudly. "I know who took it. Pierce did. He's always playing tricks on me!"

"You're impossible, Hattie," Pierce said, listening from his room down the hall. "Why would I do that?"

Hattie was ready to cry. She was sure someone in her family had taken her ring, but who? She left for school with a heavy heart.

When she came home from school, she looked everywhere. Still no ring.

The next day, it was "show and tell" time again at

She opened the treasure box. "My ring! It's gone."

school. This time, anyone who had a hobby could tell the class about it. Arnold shot up his hand.

"I want to show my stone collection," he said. He held up several polished pebbles and unusual stones he had found on his farm. Hattie leaned on her elbows. Anyone could have a dumb stone collection.

Suddenly Hattie sat up. Arnold had taken her ring! Hadn't he said he wanted the stone from her ring to add to his collection?

"Now I know who took my ring," she said, pointing her finger straight at Arnold. "The night you were at my house, you must have stolen my ring from my treasure box while I was helping Mom with the cookies and hot cocoa!"

"You're a liar," yelled Arnold angrily. "I never took your dumb ring."

"Stop quarreling," Miss Henry said. "Don't accuse anyone, Hattie, if you don't have all the facts."

Arnold muttered under his breath, "Liar."

Hattie glared at Arnold. She was sure he had taken the ring and she would prove it, too.

For the next several days, Hattie made life miserable for Arnold as she spread the word that he was a thief. The rest of the kids started avoiding Arnold, fearful that he would steal something of theirs too. Arnold was hurt and bewildered.

One evening, Hattie decided to tell her Mom and Dad what she thought had happened to her ring.

"Hattie," said Dad, "you don't know for sure that Arnold took the ring. What if he didn't take it?"

"I'm sure he did," Hattie said stubbornly.

"Don't blame anyone unless you know who did it," said Dad.

Little Ervin sat on the floor, listening to Hattie and his parents. "See ring, see ring," said Ervin. He had an imagination like Hattie's, and she seldom believed what he said. But Hattie was curious.

"What kind of a ring?" she asked.

"I show you," said Ervin. Hattie followed him into her parents' bedroom. He climbed up on the bed and looked down over the headboard. "Here," he said, as he pointed down.

Hattie pulled the bed away from the wall. There on the floor was her ring! Not only her ring, but lots of other things Ervin had collected— Kathryn's barrette, Pierce's flashlight, a bar of soap, and even the wristwatch Mom thought she had lost.

"Why did you hide all these things?" Hattie demanded as she picked up her ring.

Ervin knew Hattie was angry with him. Big tears came to his eyes. "My treasure, my treasure," he said.

Glad to have her ring back, Hattie quickly forgave Ervin. Suddenly she remembered the terrible things she had said about Arnold. And he had been so nice the night they played checkers. And now he hadn't taken her ring after all. And . . . if only she hadn't told quite so many people.

The next day at school, she knew what she had to do.

"Arnold, I found my ring," she told him with her head bowed. "I'm sorry I said you took it."

"I told you I didn't," said Arnold. "You wouldn't believe me. You told the other kids I was a thief."

Miss Henry overheard them talking. "Hattie," she suggested, "I think you have something to say to the rest of the class."

It wasn't easy to apologize to so many people at once, but Hattie knew the sooner she did it, the sooner it would be over. She stood in front of the whole class, cleared her throat, and blurted out, "I made a bad mistake about Arnold and I'm really sorry. I will never do it again."

She felt much better. That day she vowed she would never blame anybody without knowing the truth. And she had a beautiful birthstone ring to remind her.

Chapter 12

JUST
IN TIME
FOR
CHRISTMAS

*H*attie was sitting at the dining room table drawing a snowman. Dad and Pierce were playing checkers at the other end of the table. Mom and Kathryn were baking pies in the kitchen.

Outside snow was falling. It looked like a Christmas card, but Hattie did not feel like Christmas was coming. She still missed her friend Ruthie Rhenn. She wondered if Ruthie was getting ready for Christmas.

The telephone rang, and Dad went to answer it. "Hello, Mr. Rhenn. What? That's wonderful. Of course, we'll be right there."

Dad stared at the phone. Then he squeezed his eyes shut and smiled.

"What's the matter?" asked Hattie. "Ruthie's been found," he said in a choked voice, still smiling. "She's in the hospital in Worthington."

"Ruthie's been found!" shrieked Hattie. "Let's go!" Hattie took Dad's hand and pulled him toward the door.

"Hattie, Hattie," laughed Dad, "I think Ruthie can wait until we get our coats on."

Dad didn't seem to mind getting out his car to drive Hattie to Worthington. All the way Hattie kept saying over and over, "Thank you, God! Thank you for answering my prayers."

Mr. Rhenn was in the lobby when they walked into the hospital. He had a big smile on his face.

"She's right down the hall," he said as he turned to lead the way.

When he pushed open the door to Ruthie's room, Hattie ran to her friend's bed. "Oh, Ruthie," she exclaimed, "I'm so glad to see you."

Tears were shining in Ruthie's eyes. The two girls hugged each other long and hard.

"Tell us what happened. Where did the gypsies take you?" Hattie asked.

"It wasn't the gypsies," Ruthie said.

Before she could say more, Mr. Rhenn stepped forward. "No, it wasn't," he said. "I think I had better tell this part. Mrs. Rhenn and I adopted Ruthie when she was a baby. Her parents wanted to keep her, but they were poor and already had many children. Another baby was just too much for them at the time. Ruthie came to live with us right after she was born, but we never told her that she was adopted."

Ruthie sat up in bed. She held Hattie's hand as she talked. "A man drove into your yard that day while I had my eyes closed and you were hiding. He had followed us to your house on the bus from school. He tricked me into coming close to his car; then he threw me inside and raced down the road. He promised he wouldn't hurt me, but he said I had to come home with him because he was my real dad." Ruthie looked at Mr. Rhenn. "I didn't believe him—at first," she said.

"He drove to a broken-down farmhouse a long way past Worthington. A woman who said she was my mother came out of the house. It turned out that she was the one who wanted me to help with the housework.

"She untied my hands and made me start washing dishes right away. Then she had me mop the floors and change the dirty beds. I felt like Cinderella before she went to the prince's ball. I had to work hard day after day."

"Oh, Ruthie, how did you stand it?" Hattie asked. She squeezed Ruthie's hand.

"I kept hoping that one day I would escape. And I remembered that you always said where there's a

Ruthie sat up in bed. She held Hattie's hand as she talked.

will, there's a way. Two days ago I decided that if I didn't leave that place soon, I would die. I knew I had to try. I had walked a long way toward Worthington when a car stopped. A man in uniform got out and spoke to me in a loud deep voice. I just started crying, 'Please take me home. I want my mom. I want my dad.' The last thing I remember was hearing him say that he would take me to the hospital."

"That's enough for now, Ruthie," said her dad. He looked at Mr. Hart as he stepped closer to Ruthie. "She was very lucky. The man who brought her here was the sheriff, and Ruthie told the nurse who she was. The sheriff came to our house and told us. Mrs. Rhenn almost fainted when she heard the good news."

"What's going to happen to the man who kidnapped Ruthie?" Dad asked.

"The sheriff has taken care of him and his wife. We learned that she is not Ruthie's real mother. They won't be bothering anyone else." Mr. Rhenn patted Ruthie's head and smiled.

"Oh, Ruthie," said Hattie, "you're home just in time for Christmas."

"I don't have any gifts to give this year," Ruthie said.

"Yes, you do. You're our gift," Hattie replied.

"That's right," Dad said. "We want the whole Rhenn family to come to our house for Christmas Eve."

Hattie began to jump up and down with excitement, and Ruthie smiled from ear to ear.

Just then the nurse came in. "That's enough company for now, Ruthie. You need to rest if you want to go home for Christmas."

"We'll leave," said Hattie, "because we want Ruthie out of this place and at ours on Christmas Eve." She hugged Ruthie tight, and she and Dad left. Hattie danced down the hall.

Three days later the two families sat around the Christmas tree in the Harts' parlor. They had just finished a fine dinner of roast goose and all the trimmings. Mom had put her new tablecloth from the gypsies on the table. It looked so pretty.

A fire burned in the fireplace and the room smelled of fresh pine. Pierce had cut the tree the day before and Mom, Hattie, Leona, and Clarence had decorated it. Hattie loved the star on top. Kathryn had cut it out and decorated it when she was a little girl.

Dad opened his Bible and began to read the verses about the first Christmas in the second chapter of Luke. Hattie and Ruthie held hands as they listened to the lovely story. When Dad got to the part about "good news of great joy," Hattie squeezed Ruthie's hand.

After Dad finished reading, he prayed, "Thank you, God, for sending your Son into this world so that those who seek Him may find Him."

"And thank you, Lord," prayed Mr. Rhenn, "for helping us find our precious daughter."

Hattie and Ruthie opened their eyes after his prayer and gave each other a quick smile. From now on, everything would be fine. Hattie just knew it.

Experience the *Treasures of Childhood*
Growing up in a twelve-member family on a farm in the 1920s creates many opportunities for adventure and discovery. Enjoy each exciting book in the *Treasures of Childhood* series as young Hattie Hart explores the magnificent world around her and learns important value lessons in the process.

Hattie's Faraway Family
Hattie volunteers to drive Mrs. Lynn to Worthington—even though she's never driven before. Then, baby Elmer disappears at the beach when she is suppose to be watching him. These adventures and others teach Hattie the importance of responsibility.

Hattie's Holidays
Hattie sneaks out of the house on her birthday to try out her new skates—and breaks her ankle! Then, she lights a candle and accidentally sets the Christmas tree on fire. Through these experiences, Hattie learns the hard way that rules are not to spoil her fun, but to protect her.

Hattie's Adventures
Her best friend gets stranded on the roof when Hattie and her brothers take away the ladder she used to get up. Then, Hattie thinks up a dirty trick to get even with her brother for a prank he pulled on her. Through all the teasing, they learn to laugh together and appreciate each other.

All titles are available at your favorite Christian bookstore.